An Old Time Cl

Written by Tom Christopher

Illustrated by Heather Reilly

Published by Reilly Books
At Createspace
www.reillybooks.com

ISBN: 9781515122111

This book is dedicated to the child inside us all. As we grow older, memories of Christmas time when we were children become nearer and dearer to us. Christmas keeps the child in us all alive.

And for Dayanara and Nevaeh, your smiles are like Christmas tree lights that brighten up the room. Let this be the first of many stories that begin: "when I was your age..."

Watching a Christmas show with my son,

On a snowy Christmas Eve.

He asked "Daddy is Santa real?

Do you and mom still believe?"

I stayed up one Christmas Eve

To see if it was true,

To find out if Santa was real,

That's what I'd hoped to do.

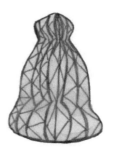

Don't know how he got there,

His beard was white, his belly was big,

There he was working away,

Dancing and doing a jig.

"I's the b'y that brings the toys,

Stuffs the stockings like ya would,

For all the nice little boys and girls

That are some shockin' good."

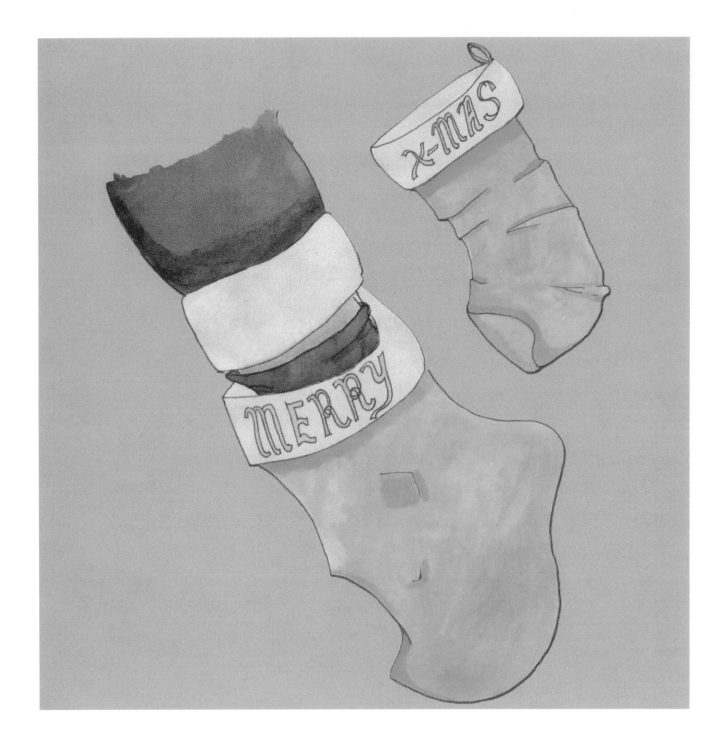

"I gets all that I can eat
And clingy me son, to spare.
To top it off I only work
One night out of the year."

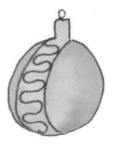

It took a minute to realize,

I soon came to understand,

Not only is Santa real,

He's also from Newfoundland.

He finished up the work at hand,

To the back porch he did go,

Laced his logan's good and tight

Before walking through the snow.

He made his way on down the road,

I'll never forget the sight.

A komatik sled, and eight Newfoundland dogs

Disappeared into the night.

Bios

Tom Christopher has been writing poetry and song lyrics for almost a decade. He began by writing poetry for his own enjoyment, and when it was discovered and loved by others, he began writing music for the albums of a local music group: DaNdA. His first book, *Santa Almost Missed Our Town*, was originally one of the group's songs from a Christmas album. *An Old Time Christmas*, was written as a poem after a taping for a Christmas special, and has been brought to life here for your enjoyment.

Heather is the author of three medieval fantasy novels in a series called the *Binding of the Almatraek*. She has also written and illustrated three other books for young children. With a background as a music teacher, she often emphasizes the use of rhyme or cadence in her books, and includes activities at the end that parents, caregivers, and teachers can use with their children. She currently lives in Dildo, Newfoundland, with her husband, two small children.

Other Books by Tom Christopher:

Santa Almost Missed Our Town

Albums Featuring Lyrics/Songs:

D aNd A Vault One,

D aNd A "Yes Me Buddy"

D aNd A Christmas Vault Two

Learn more about the author's music at:

www.danda2010.com

Other books written and illustrated by Heather Reilly:

Novels:

Binding of the Almatraek Book I: *Knight's Surrender*
Binding of the Almatraek Book II: *Noble Pursuit*
Binding of the Almatraek Book III: *Enchanted Page*

Children's:

The Tree and the Sun
Tock-Tick-Tock, the Mouse and the Clock
The Poetical Alphabetical Book

Upcoming books:

The Rat of Redvine
The Words We See: *Kindergarten Sight Words on the Rock*

Learn more about the illustrator and her books at:

www.reillybooks.com

Made in the USA
Charleston, SC
17 September 2015